Dealing with Negative Emotions

Bonnie L. Bair

Life Improvements 2

Galesburg, Illinois

Names: Bair, Bonnie L. | Bair, Bonnie

Title: Dealing with Negative Emotions

Description: 1st edition | Galesburg; Illinois: Life Improvements 2, 2021

Subject: How to deal with negative emotions

Identifiers: LCCN 2021918127 print

ISBN 978-0-9994772-8-1

Dealing with Negative Emotions

Table of Contents

Dealing with Negative Emotions

Sadness/Grief, ***Betrayal***, Guilt, **Embarrassment**, Depression, **ANXIETY/Worry**, **Fear**, Loneliness, **Frustration/Anger**

Our emotions and Other's Emotions

1. Identify/Acknowledge it.
2. Normalize it.

How we were raised has a lot to do with how we might deal with emotions. For example: Were we allowed to express our feelings?
Were we allowed to say "No" to our parents?
Were we punished for how we behaved when we felt different feelings? What was the message we got about those feelings?
Do we feel like we are bad when we feel negative feelings?

When we feel negative emotions, it is common to turn those inward and start to see ourselves as failures. The following are thoughts we can use to

build ourselves up when experiencing negative feelings. Using them regularly will help us deal with the
negative more effectively and help us to have more positive feelings.

Thought Patterns to overcome Self-hate:

I'm forgiven and loved.
I'm accepting of myself.
I enjoy being me.
I ask for what I want and need with ease.
I am fearfully and wonderfully made in God's image. Psalm 39:13-14
I am saved through faith in Christ Jesus.

Sadness/Grief can have a variety of causes; namely the loss of something or someone.

Sadness can also be caused by someone doing or not doing something, that causes a person grief.

Sadness dissipates when we acknowledge the loss and sadness. Time also helps to heal. Helping someone else in their time of need can also help us to heal from ours. Exercise and eating healthy foods can keep us from entering a long-lasting depression.

Betrayal is one of the more difficult feelings to recover from. When a trusted friend, spouse, or other family member betrays us, it can be difficult to recover from.

How to handle it when someone sins against you.

Go to them and discuss it with them and no other person. Matthew 18:15-19

If they listen, that's great! If not, consider taking someone else with you to discuss it with them.

Pray for your enemies. Ask God to convict them of their sin and help them to turn and repent, and stop and understand their behavior, so they can receive God's love and have better relationships with others and a better life. Consider doing something nice for them or saying something true and nice about them.

Love your enemies. Bless them that curse you. Do good to them that hate you and pray for them which despitefully use you and persecute you. Matthew 5:43-47

You might consider speaking with the person and your Pastor about the situation, if necessary. Finally, sometimes it's best to let it go and guard yourself against further hurt.

Guilt

How to Deal with Guilt,

Acknowledge Sin. Apologize and ask for forgiveness.

If we confess our sins, He who is faithful and just, will forgive us our sins and cleanse us from all unrighteousness. 1 John 1:9

What to do if someone tries to make you feel guilty?

Tell yourself the truth. **Is it because?**

A. They need/want, or think they need/want something from you? – Let your Yes be Yes and your No, No.
B. An Apology? – Put yourself in their shoes and try to see things from their perspective.

C. A Thank you? – Ask or keep in mind what kind of things they value, such as hugs, gifts, words of acknowledgment, time, or acts of service, and pair those with the thank you. This will make your acknowledgment of their efforts more heartfelt, to them.

D. Your Company? - Try pre-scheduling time with them, so they have something to look forward to and will know when they will see you again. Take advantage of technology and schedule regular facetime calls (when it's difficult to see each other in person).

E. They want your help in repairing a relationship? If you are uncomfortable doing so, tell them. Just as they want your understanding, you can ask them to be understanding of you as well. If you are willing to help, do so. Ask them to be more direct in asking or in stating their needs. Tell them when they do so, it will help you respond more appropriately to them, rather than getting mad. Remember, you both have choices.

F. They want your help? – If you choose not to help because of other priorities you have, just tell them you have some other things you need to take care of. Offer to do what you can and tell them they will need to find another option besides you. You can only do what you can do and if you are not willing, it will be bad for the relationship, or another of your relationships, in the long run. Ask God for wisdom and direction with this and do as God tells you to do. Pray for the person that's asking. God will help meet their need.

G. They have a bad habit of making other people feel guilty? – In a kind tone of voice, ask: "You're not trying to make me feel guilty, are you? (Idea from Brian Tracy) Doing so, will help them realize their behavior and adjust accordingly.

Examples of ways to respond when someone is trying to make you feel guilty.

1. "I like when you simply ask for what you need and want."

2. "I like spending time with you when it is at a time that is mutually beneficial to both of us and /or when we do things, we both enjoy."

3. "I must have not thanked you in a way in which you valued, or I must have not acknowledged your efforts in a way you desired."

If you think someone is trying to get you to do something you do not want to do:

Remember, you have choices. No one can make you do something you do not want to do.

Ask yourself: Am I listening to what they are saying? Am I interrupting? Am, I judging them?

Are they being selfish? Or do they just want me to listen, understand or acknowledge them?

If you don't want to have anything to do with what they are saying, but want to respond lovingly:

1. Listen without interrupting or without jumping to conclusions.
2. Try telling the other person what you think they are saying - ask questions or listen more closely to make sure you understand correctly.
3. Summarize what you think they are saying and ask if that is what they are saying.
4. Respond by saying "No", using a confident yet loving tone.
5. Stating your preference, or needs can help the other person understand and can improve the relationship.

<u>What to do when you perceive the other person as your enemy:</u> something doesn't look, sound, or seem (smell right, so to speak) right.

1. You might want to check it out and ask questions to make sure you haven't jumped to the wrong conclusion.
2. Pray for wisdom for yourself and pray for them.
3. Ask God to convict them of their sin and help them with the struggles that cause them to trouble you.

Ask God to save their soul, if he hasn't already. Ask God to show you if there is something that needs adjusting in your attitude and behavior.

4. Recognize and say something true and good about them or to them. Or just go about your business and don't let it bother you. Treat them as a tax collector or unbeliever.

What to do when you have a disagreement or disagree with someone.

1. Agree with what you can agree on.
2. You might agree to disagree. Or agree to give it some time before discussing again.

Try thinking: I look for something I can agree /or help with.

1. I acknowledge the other person's feelings and needs and tell them what I heard them say or what I understand them to need.
2. I do and say what I'm willing to do and I ask God to do the rest.
3. If I am unable or I am unwilling to help, I say so. It's ok to say No when you need to.

Accepting Responsibility for our thinking and speech will change our lives in the direction we desire. It is up to US/God. If not:

Why did God give us free will?

Why did God create us in God's image?

Why did God create us each to be unique?

Why did God say to delight in God and God will give us the desires of our hearts?

Why did Jesus say, if you remain in me and my words remain in you, you can ask for whatever you want, and it will be done for you by my Father in Heaven?

Embarrassment is one of those feelings that can be hard to shake, especially if others do not let you live it down, so to speak.

When I was a senior in high school, I was the new kid on the block. It was my second week at my new school. I was in outdoor living class on a fishing trip when I sunk knee-deep into the ground. I was wearing my bright yellow pants (this was in the eighties), white socks, and penny loafers. I was able to slip my feet out of my penny loafers to free my feet from the thick, sticky mud. I had to dig with my hands to retrieve my shoes. As I washed my arms and legs at the water pump, I was surrounded by classmates with looks of disbelief. It was quite embarrassing. I laughed, so I wouldn't cry. This event could have been detrimental as a new student at school. However, I was fortunate it did not hurt me. The other students then had something to talk with me about. I am thankful for their graciousness. I wonder how they might have reacted if I had gotten upset about the event. Would it then be funny to them? Perhaps, because I could see the humor in the situation and laugh at myself, it was easier for us all to deal with.

This type of embarrassment is different than the kind when a person does/says something they are ashamed of, in the presence of other people. I guess I would say, first, ask God for forgiveness and then go to each person, if possible, and acknowledge the mistake and ask for understanding and forgiveness. This should help make sure the mistake does not follow you, for what may seem like forever.

Depression can happen when we get down on ourselves or our life situation.

Ways to Overcome Depression

Things to Consider:

Talking with God. Asking God to show or tell you why you have been depressed.

Seek information about depression: Google it, Talk with Doctor/Expertise, Read a Book.

Assess the depressing thoughts. Is there something your mind has often wandered to or things you have often been depressed about? What have been the triggers or what could be the cause/s of the depression? A loss, or losses? Lack of sleep? A side effect of the medication? Poor diet or nutrition? Unhappy relationship? Injury or pain? Is it another health issue? Or is it a combination of things?

Ask someone for something you want and need. Avoid isolation.

Speak to the relevant people, about the things that are bothering you, as soon as possible.

Keep Prayer Journal to keep track of answered prayers for encouragement. Keep Prayer Journal to keep track of answered prayers for encouragement.

Talk with a friend or Counselor.

Attend a grief support group or another relevant support group.

Sleep Apnea evaluation/treatment - since lack of quality sleep can contribute to depression. – (A person can have sleep apnea, even if they don't snore.)

Ask your spouse or another person to address issues that concern you.

Consider a pet or emotional support animal to take care of and cuddle or play with.

Consider reading the bible or a devotional daily for encouragement and peace.

Try listening to music or soothing sounds (such as waves, rain, birds, etc.).

Put the phone on night mode in the evening so you don't excite your mind before trying to sleep and turn off other electronics 1 hour before sleep time.

Keep a short to-do list to help motivate you without overwhelming you. If you think of something, during the night (you are concerned you will forget) get out of bed and write it down.

Create a plan for addressing any concerns you have or have had, for a long time.

Call a friend or family member that you enjoy talking and spending time with.

Avoid saying things like: "I feel so depressed." And "It's getting worse all the time." (When talking with other people.) Instead, you might try saying: "I have been feeling depressed and it has been getting worse lately."

Practice deep breathing, Kegels, and affirmations such as: *"I am okay." "I know what to do." I can do all things through Christ who gives me strength." "Today is a new day." "New opportunities come my way."*

Try doing something different and fun, to give your mind a vacation.

Consider using essential oils, meditation, or Tai Chi

Consider herbs such as Ashwagandha, Holy Basil, or St. John's Wort, along with some type of Omega 3 like fish, flax, or hemp oil. The combination can be effective in reducing depression. Do Research! Cross-reference with other meds and health conditions when searching on google. Ask your doctor!

Consider taking magnesium and vitamin D, as low levels can cause depression. The need for supplemental vitamins increases in the winter, due to less available sunlight and time in the sun. **Do your research! – google it. Ask God and Doctor!**

Increasing activity level usually decreases depression. Try completing activity 2 hours before sleep time or earlier in the day, so it doesn't interfere with sleep.

Maintain as regular of a wake-sleep schedule/routine as you can.

Stay away from unnecessary drugs and alcohol – It will only compound troubles in the long run. Consider nutrients or herbs/seeing a Counselor, instead.

Limit electronics in the bedroom to only special times such as a movie during a storm, etc. Preferably, eliminate TV and electronics from the bedroom. Lack of quality sleep can increase anxiety levels.

Talk with someone who used to have depression to get ideas, information, and encouragement from them.

Adjust your life (choices, priorities, & schedule), as needed.

Consider diet changes to support your mental/physical health.

Get help from professionals, as needed, to help with health, money, and relationship issues.

Consider medicine, if necessary. Check out your options and side effects. Research!

Consider attending a class.

Ask for prayer. Forgive yourself.

Practice breathing while closing your eyes and visualizing a happy place or time.

Ask God for forgiveness and wisdom – God gives wisdom liberally to those who ask.

Practice self-talk like: "I am loved, accepted, and forgiven."

Make plans to spend time with a friend or family member each day or week, as needed.

Go to church, a play, or a concert. Watch something different on TV. Learn something new. Try to always have something to look forward to.

Connect with an old friend on Facebook or join a Facebook group.

Do something to help someone else.

Do something you've always have wanted to do. Ask someone to do it with you or do it by yourself.

Try looking at things from another perspective - like a dog's, or a bird's, or a bug's perspective.

Go see a movie or treat yourself to dinner.

Eat food & drink water and take nutrients to support your mind and body.

Avoid processed foods, omega 6's like hydrogenated oils, sugar, and alcohol.

Think the best of yourself and others.

Pray for others and yourself.

Get adequate rest and exercise.

Take inventory of what you have been watching and listening to. Have these things been contributing to your unhappiness? Try going without them and doing, watching, and listening to something else.

Concentrate on something/s or someone you are thankful for.

If thinking about death or ending your life*, call your doctor or tell someone who can look out for you and know what to do, right away. If you cannot get a hold of them: call your doctor, go to the emergency room, or call a suicide prevention hotline.* ***Get treatment as soon as possible!*** *Update doctor of any noticeable changes right away. Schedule and attend follow-up appointments.*

Consider sharing a house or an apartment, if lonely or in need of help with paying the bills.

Do whatever you can to make sure you are safe and around someone who will look out for your interest! **Stay with a friend or ask them to stay with you.**

Get treatment for depression as soon as possible, so it doesn't get worse! And so, you can have a better life!

National Suicide Prevention Lifeline (800) 273-8255

ANXIETY/Worry

Ways to Overcome Anxiety *by Life Improvements, PLLC*

Anxiety is an indicator (like a yellow light) of something needing to be done.

Things to Consider:

Talking with God. Asking God to show or tell you why you have been so anxious.

Seek information about anxiety: Google it, Talk with Doctor/Expertise, Read a Book.

Assess your anxious thoughts. Is there something your mind has often wandered to or things you have often worried about? What triggers have there been?

Ask someone for something you want and need. Talk with a friend or Counselor.

Sleep Apnea evaluation/treatment, since lack of quality sleep, can cause anxiety. (A person can have sleep apnea, even if they don't snore.)

Ask your spouse or another person to address health issues that concern you.

Consider a pet or emotional support animal.

Consider reading the bible or a devotional daily for encouragement and peace.

Try listening to music or soothing sounds (such as waves, rain, birds, etc.).

Put the phone on night mode in the evening so you don't excite your mind before trying to sleep and turn off other electronics 1 hour before sleep time.

Speak to the relevant people, about the things that are bothering you, as soon as possible.

Keep Prayer Journal or to-do list. If you think of something, during the night (you are concerned you will forget) get out of bed and write it down.

Create a plan for addressing any concerns you have or have had, for a long time.

Practice deep breathing, Kegels, and affirmations such as: *"I pray, smile, and relax, so I achieve the max." "I'm okay." "I know*

***what to do, I know exactly what to do!"* "I pray, do my best, and I trust God for the rest."**

Avoid saying things like: "I worry a lot." (When talking with other people.) Instead, you might try saying: "In the past, I've worried a lot."

Cut down on or avoid caffeine and artificial sweeteners. They are known to cause anxiety.

Try doing something different and fun, to give your mind a break.

Consider using essential oils, meditation, or Tia Chi

Consider herbs such as Ashwagandha, or Holy Basil, along with some type of Omega 3 like fish, flax, or hemp oil. The combination can be very effective in reducing anxiety.

Consider taking magnesium and vitamin D, as low levels can cause anxiety. Do your research – google it, ask God and Doctor.

Increasing activity levels may reduce stress/anxiety. Try completing activity 2 hours before sleep time or earlier in the day, so it doesn't interfere with sleep.

Maintain as regular of a wake-sleep schedule/routine as you can.

Stay away from unnecessary drugs and alcohol – It will only compound troubles in the long run. Consider nutrients or herbs/seeing a Counselor, instead.

Limit electronics in the bedroom to only special times such as a movie during a storm, etc. Preferably, eliminate TV and electronics from the bedroom. Lack of quality sleep can increase anxiety levels.

Talk with someone who used to have high anxiety to get ideas, information, and encouragement from them.

Adjust your life (choices, priorities, & schedule), as needed.

Consider medicine, if necessary. Check out your options and side effects. Research!

Do whatever you can to address anxiety. Without attention, it will get worse and cause problems in your life and relationships!

Ways to Stop Excessive Working, Spending, Eating, TV, Hoarding, Gaming, Addictions, Etc.

***Things to Consider*:**

Seek information about the issue: Talk to God & Ask for Wisdom, who gives liberally to those who ask. Google the issue. Talk/Listen to someone who cares. Doctor or Expert. Read a Book.

Ask yourself: How much of this is due to worry?

1. Pray whenever worried about something & ask God for help
2. Do gentle Kegels, with any worrying thoughts
3. Omega 3's like hemp, flax, or fish oil; along with Ashwagandha or Holy Basil (google and research!)
4. Affirmations

Ask Yourself: How much of this is due to loneliness?

1. Pray
2. Consider: getting a roommate or pet, calling someone to see how they are and how they are doing and asking if you can help them with something, asking a friend (or someone you like) to do something with you.

Ask Yourself: How much of this is due to stress?

1. Pray

2. Assess the Source of Stress.

   If Clutter: De-clutter! Look for the easiest thing to start with, then the next, and keep going. Take breaks as you need.

   If too many things to do: Prioritize. Start with the most logical or easiest. Delegate. Ask for help. Change plans or target date.

   If too much information: Read or deal with one thing at a time.

Consider fasting Facebook, the news, TV, or radio. Unsubscribe to unnecessary email. Consider reading, or asking for, a summary.

If someone is causing you stress: Talk with them. Ask for cooperation. If they are unwilling, spend less time with them. Spend more time with friends/family who comforts and encourage you. Practice gentle Kegels or belly breathing w stress.

Ask Yourself: How much is due to problems in my relationships?

1. Pray. Ask God for what you want and need.
2. Do Research: Bible, Google, "We Smile" book.
3. Repent/Repair.

Ask Yourself: How much of this is due to boredom?

1. Pray and ask God for an idea or direction.
2. Consider: Creating a list of things to do for reference at times when you get bored. calling a friend or family member and seeing how they are, taking up a hobby, clearing out the cupboards, doing something for someone else, reading something, researching something to help you or someone else.

Ask Yourself: How much of this is due to sadness?

1. Talk to God.
2. Consider: Telling yourself the truth. Kegels. Align your speech with scripture. Feel the sadness, so it will dissipate. Take a bath. Massage your feet. Talk with a friend or a Counselor. Do some activity that will increase endorphins. Listen to some uplifting or energetic music. Say affirmations. Encourage/Listen to someone else.

Watch a movie or something funny. Get some rest. Do something different or interesting. Join a support group.

3. Research nutrients to support your body – Omega 3's, Ashwagandha, Vitamin D, Magnesium, and L-methyl-folate.
4. Talk to your Doctor. Consider medicine. Do your research. Report any concerns to the doctor right away for medicine change or adjustment. Follow-up with Doctor/Counselor.

Ask Yourself: How much excessiveness is due to my <u>physical health</u>?

1. Pray and ask for wisdom. Ask elders of the church to anoint w/oil and pray for you.
2. Do research. Google how to treat the condition
3. See a doctor, if needed.
4. Ask someone else who has or has had, a similar issue, to see what they have

tried and what has been helpful to them.
5. Do what is required to get better.
6. Get physical activity/rehab without making the issue worse.
7. Adjust what and how much you eat/drink. Try to get 32 oz of water per day.
8. Swap alcohol for special non-alcoholic drinks you will enjoy.
9. Research/consider nutrients like Omega 3's, Vitamin D, Magnesium, Vitamin C, etc.

Ask Yourself: How much of this is due to not being in a relationship with w/someone special?

1. Pray. Ask God for what you want and for direction.
2. Attend a class, an event, or church to meet new people.
3. Ask someone you like to do something with you or help them with something.

4. Ask friends/family if they know someone who might be interested in meeting you.

Ask yourself if it's due to <u>too many people suffering or needing help around you</u>?

1. Pray. Ask God for Wisdom. Pray for whenever/whoever comes to your mind. Ask God to let you know if there is something specific God wants you to do for them and do whatever he says and when. Otherwise, let it go.
2. Limit Facebook time. Let others be responsible for themselves or find someone else to help them. Arrange specific times that work for you to interact with others. Schedule downtime to take care of yourself and do something fun.
3. When someone asks or needs something of you, do what you can without putting yourself at risk or causing problems for yourself.

4. Say "No" when you want/need to (in a loving way!) Only say "Yes," when you want to.

Ask Yourself: How much of this is due to a <u>bad habit</u>?

1. Talk to God. Acknowledge the habit and ask for forgiveness. Ask for wisdom and help in making changes. Pray for your God to keep you from temptation and deliver you from evil each day. Be thankful and count your blessings.
2. Create a Specific Simple Plan
3. Write an Affirmation. Place it on your bathroom mirror, in your phone with a reminder alarm, or your dashboard. Say it out loud for 1-2 minutes a day.
4. Come up with a replacement activity or technique to reduce the habit.
5. Set Goals and Reward your progress!
6. Keep away from temptation such as stores, candy aisle, certain websites, keep yourself busy with other

activities, eat with your non-dominate hand, increase your water or vegetable intake, read the bible, etc.

7. Select someone who will help you be accountable and who will encourage you.

Ask Yourself: How much of this is due to <u>spiritual oppression (the devil)?</u>

1. Pray. Then say, "I resist a spirit of depression, gluttony, infirmity, fear, greed, jealousy, or idolatry, etc., and oppression, in the name of Jesus Christ." Say, "Satan, you must go and not return to me in the name of Jesus Christ." Then ask God to replace what had been taken, with a spirit of joy, peace, health, courage, generosity, faithfulness, and freedom, in the Name of Jesus Christ."
2. Thank God for it.
3. Trust it to be taken care of it and do something in faith that lines up with what you have asked God for it.

Insomnia can happen that when we are experiencing negative feelings, especially WORRY.

The following are Ways to Overcome Insomnia/Sleep Issues *by Life Improvements, PLLC*

Things to Consider:

Talking with God. Asking God to show or tell you why you have been having sleep issues.

Seek information about sleep: Google, Talk with Doctor/Expertise, Read a Book

Assess your thoughts at night. Is there something your mind often wanders to or dreams about

Ask someone for something you want and need.

Sleep Apnea Evaluation/Treatment or other Health Issues.

Asking your spouse or another person to get treated for snoring or any other health issue that interferes with your sleep. If they are unwilling. Ask them to sleep in another room or consider sleeping in another room yourself.

Consider temperature, lighting, sound, scheduling issues to be adjusted.

Consider running an air purifier at night or during the day in your bedroom.

Consider another solution to kids/dogs sleeping in bed with you.

Body Pillow or heat, cold pack for comfort or pain relief.

Turn off all electronics 1 hour before bedtime.

Put your phone in night mode in the evening so you don't excite your mind before trying to sleep.

Try listening to instrumental music, white noise (such as fan, waves, rain, birds, etc.), or affirmations of your choice (said by you or someone else), as you fall to sleep or throughout the night.

Keep Prayer Journal or to-do list in the bathroom. If you think of something you are concerned you will forget, get out of bed and write it down.

Speak to the relevant people, about the things that are bothering you, as soon as possible.

Create a plan for addressing any difficulties you may be or have had for quite some time – at a time other than sleep time.

Practice deep breathing, Kegels, and affirmations such as: "I relax and sleep now." "I sleep like a baby."

Avoid saying things like: "I don't sleep well." Or "I can't sleep." (When talking with other people.) Instead, you might try saying: "I haven't been sleeping well." Or "In the past, I haven't slept well."

Avoid caffeine altogether. Or cut down on the amount and limit it to the first half of your day.

Keep any naps to less than 20 minutes a day, so it doesn't interfere with nighttime sleep.

Consider using essential oils, chamomile tea, holy basil, medicine, or other nutrients to help you fall and stay asleep.

Consider activity level during the day. Increasing activity level may be helpful in feelings of tiredness at sleep time and with sleep-wake cycles. Try completing activity 2 hours before sleep time or earlier in the day to allow for a wind downtime.

If you have 3rd shift or varying shift work, consider asking the doctor for meds to help with adjustment and napping when you can.

Maintain as regular of a wake-sleep schedule/routine as you can.

Stay away from unnecessary drugs and alcohol – It will only compound troubles in the long run. Consider nutrients or herbs/seeing a Counselor, instead.

Limit electronics in the bedroom to only special times such as a movie during a storm, etc. Preferably, eliminate TV and electronics from the bedroom.

Talk with someone who used to have insomnia to get ideas, information, and encouragement from them.

Adjustments to your life (choices, priorities, & schedule), as needed.

Lack of sleep contributes to anxiety/depression and problems in relationships!

FEAR

I learned from Minister Kate McVeigh that Fear is False Evidence Appearing Real

Although it is normal to feel scared at times and fear can be a flag for attending to something immediate; fear causes us to be cautious. It is different from...worry in that fear may grip us or be a warning to us to take a different path.

We need to assess if the fear is holding us back or a warning to do something different. Faith is the opposite of fear. God does not give us a spirit of fear but of power love and a sound mind (1 Timothy 1:7). In this instance, if we are fearful of doing something we want to do, that is probably not from God. Faith is the opposite of fear. Faith comes from hearing the word of God. Fear can be a healthy fear that warns us and keeps us safe. However, a spirit of fear will keep us from experiencing blessing and doing the things we would like to do. That is spiritual oppression. It keeps us from obtaining God's promises or blessings in our lives. If you are a Christian and believe in God's resurrection power through Christ Jesus, you can tell a spirit of fear to leave you in the name of Jesus Christ and it must obey you. You have authority, as a believer to do this and free yourself from bondage to fear.

If you are lacking faith in this, read the Bible out loud. Faith comes from hearing the word of God (2 Corinthians 5:17).

Loneliness is one of the most difficult emotions because one often feels isolated from others, draws inwards, and spirals downward into self-pity and depression. It is so important to try your best to connect with others. Be a friend to someone in need. Volunteer. Attend church, concerts, classes. Talk to God more. God will be there for you and/or will provide others to keep you company.

Frustration is commonly experienced before feeling Anger.

Frustration is felt when there are misunderstandings with others or when you are unable to do the things you want to do or use to do. It also happens when there are unmet expectations or needs – leading to disappointment and sometimes anger.

Minimizing frustrations as best as you can, will help keep anger away. Having realistic expectations of yourself and others will help too. Things such as repeated scheduling difficulties and miscommunications (due to not having enough time, etc.) can be decreased by better time management, or simply doing fewer activities. Taking time to rest and making time for God and his word can help one prioritize life and lessen frustrations.

They say **anger** is a secondary emotion that follows the other emotions we have been discussing.

Anger is a warning indicator light like your engine light on your vehicle. It requires immediate acknowledgment and attention. It's like an alarm. If you ignore it, bad things can happen. For example, if you ignore your alarm clock, you might be late for work and get fired. If you ignore a fire alarm, you may get burned. (In rare instances it may be important to ignore if the anger response has become a habit or gets worse with attention).

Alarms are created and set for a reason. Anger is our/others' alarm system.

The alarm of anger signifies there is danger of a perceived or real threat to a system, either internal or external. Anger is valid and requires acknowledgment and attention.

Unexplained or frequent uncontrolled anger usually signifies:

A. ***When something is going on within the system (the person) itself.***

   - More than likely, nutrients are depleted and the body is not functioning as it's designed. It is malfunctioning and is especially sensitive to certain triggers and is more susceptible to stress.

   - As nutrients are replenished, the person will heal.

B. ***When anger happens with a particular trigger*** - This signifies an *adjustment in perception or communication* is needed.

Ask yourself:

1. Is the anger due to the *continual ignoring* of concerns within your*self* or the expressed concerns of *others*?

2. Is the anger due to: Not asking? Not telling? Not caring? Not apologizing?

3. Or does the anger happen because of being too busy or having too many distractions and interruptions?

4. Does the anger stem from a lack of preparation?

5. How much of the anger is from frustration from someone perceiving you as bad or yourself perceiving someone else or yourself as bad.

6. Or is the anger from misunderstandings – of what you or someone else said, meant, or did?

How to Manage Your Anger – Breathe & Kegel

1. Stop/Assess the cause(s) of anger
2. Make sure internal systems are working properly.

\

3. Replenish the body
    - Consider nutrients (such as omega 3's, vitamins, eating different foods, herbs that help with stress or mood-stabilizing nutrients or medication.
    - Do your research!
    - Ask an expert
4. Take care of your body!
5. Practice Relaxation – Breathing & Kegels
6. Practice Purposeful Thinking.
7. Prepare for/or avoid triggers.
8. Follow the plan.

If something happens unexpectedly and requires emergent action – Ask for help!

If there is a difference in opinion between you and someone else, stop breathe and think. Do not do something you are not okay with or that you are unwilling to do! You have permission to say "No." There is a reason for the unwillingness. Ask the other person to address your concern, before agreeing or proceeding. Be willing to address the other person/s concerns, as well.

When anger happens in response to *frequent stimuli,* that happens at *expected and unexpected times.*

Prepare ahead of time.

1. Your thinking
2. Your response strategy

Examples: If you prepare for others to be clueless or inconsiderate, you will not get as upset.

If you prepare for losing track of your keys or phone, you will pay more attention to where you put them, or you will assign them a special place where you can easily find them and make a habit of placing them there regularly.

If you prepare for misunderstandings and for doing something difficult together, you will communicate more clearly and kindly.

If you prepare for hunger/crabbiness, you will keep snacks on hand.

C. **When anger happens in response to frequent ignoring or lack of cooperation.** If you've tended to get angry with others because they haven't typically listened or cooperated with you:

1. Talk to the person/people about this.
    a. Ask them what you might do to adjust and gain their ear so they can listen/or cooperate with you.

    b. Tell them you will be willing to continue to listen and cooperate with them, as they are willing to listen and cooperate with you.

2. Consider doing something different than usual, that gets their attention. Surprise them with a gift or special act of service or outing.

3. Try speaking the love language of the other person.

If you have spoken their love language and they continue to show little to no interest in speaking yours, try telling them you will do x, or won't do x, if they continue to disrespect you. Then follow through with your warning.

D. If someone frequently gets snippy with you and this causes you anger:

1. Ask the person about their expectations, such as their likes/dislikes/preferences
2. Establish Boundaries or Rules – Write them down for reference. This will establish peace, trust, and enjoyment.
3. Communicate your needs/concerns
4. Look for and negotiate win/win solutions.
    a. Focus on the goal of each person.
    b. Find a way that's acceptable to both of you. (There are usually multiple ways of doing things.) Take turns, if needed.
    c. Ask for help, if necessary.

Forgiveness

Is it ok to get angry? **Yes**, but do not let the anger stay for long, so you don't become bitter.

Forgiveness is another way we can deal with anger. It is a choice. Forgiveness sets us and the other person free. If we remember this, it will help us to move past an offense by acknowledging it and then choosing to forget it.

Does forgiveness mean allowing someone to hurt us over and over? No.

What would help you forgive someone?

Is there anyone who has hurt you that you would like an apology from?

What would you like them to say or do to help you forgive them?

Should you feel bad about expecting someone to acknowledge/change their behavior? No.

Should you feel bad about asking them? No.

Have they already apologized, but not in the way you expected or were hoping for?

How to Forgive Someone Else?

First, think the best of the other person. Remember everyone makes mistakes.

Secondly, go to the person and tell them what they did that hurt you. If it's severe or has happened often, feel free to ask them to do something to help make up for the offense – to help you forgive them and help them not repeat the behavior.

Restitution

-Repayment when damages have occurred

-May be necessary in cases of blatant disrespect or when damages are severe.

Benefits of Restitution

- Increases learning of correct behavior
- Increases respect
- Increases right behavior

When we are hurting in our attempt to love someone else, things are out of balance. We are loving our neighbor more than ourselves, not as ourselves.

Tips for Dealing with Unmet Expectations

1. Perceive/Acknowledge Good in the Other Person

    -Think from the other person's point of view.

    -Think of their feelings/needs

    -Think of their challenges/experiences

    -Check it out before jumping to conclusions

2. Eliminate words like; should, always, and never. They imply judgment. Instead use words like; sometimes, often, and rarely. They seem more truthful and will help with understanding, acceptance, and cooperation.

*It is usually in our best interest to choose to forgive and forget the offense, regardless of their behavior, to save ourselves from bitterness.

Here are some communication formulas we can follow to help deal with negative emotions and overcome challenges:

2 Step Communication Formula:

I'm feeling ______________________.

I need ___________________________.

4 Step Communication Formula:

"I feel _______ (feeling word). "

"I like when______."

"I need or would like ______."

"Would you be willing to _____?"

4 Step Communication Example 1

1. ***"I feel** frustrated."*
2. ***"I like when** the house is kept clean because it helps me function better and experience less anxiety."*
3. ***"I need** help keeping the house clean."*
4. ***"Would you be willing to** put things back where they belong? Or **would you be willing to** help me establish a home for certain items that we can agree on?"*

4 step Communication – Example 2

1. ***"I feel** sad."*
2. ***"I like when** you think the best of me."*
3. ***"I need** understanding."*
4. ***"Would you be willing to** listen to understand what I am saying?"*

Response Examples

> *"Yes, I need some time to calm down and get something to eat first."*
>
> *"Do you mind if we talk about this after supper? That will help me listen better."*

It's also a good idea to check out what the other person is thinking and feeling.

"I'm thinking you are thinking ____ *about* _____.

> ***Is that what you're thinking?"***

"I'm thinking you are feeling ____ *about* _______.

> ***Is that what you're feeling?"***

"I'm thinking you are saying or needing _______.

> ***Am I correct?"***

Another way to check things out w/example

> "***I see you*** ____ *(pulling your hair)".*
>
> ***"I hear*** ___________ *(the frustration in your voice)."*

"I think you might need ______ *(a break)."*

"Is that what you need?"

Checking with the other person about what they are thinking and feeling, helps to minimize misunderstanding and reduces the occurrence of negative feelings, or more negative feelings.

It's also important to create effective thought patterns for reaching your goals and optimal health. Choosing the thoughts you think, will help to manage the emotions of yourself and others.

Next are some examples of thought patterns that can help to manage negative emotions.

Thoughts to conquer challenges

I am responsible for my thoughts, and responses.

I speak well of others and practice positive self-talk.

I am understanding and kind.

I allow others to be who they are.

I'm responsible for my life and choices and I allow others to do the same.

I let go of hurts, allow myself to grieve, and move forward.

I think before I respond. I communicate clearly.

I ask for what I want and need with ease.

I think about what I am thankful for.

I serve others when I can do so with a smile.

I open myself to humor, friendship, and love.

I seek and attract mutually satisfying relationships with family and friends.

I create win/win solutions with others.

Dealing with Emotions Summary

1. IDENTIFY **Internal** Stimuli/Situations that Trigger Certain Emotions

    A. *Seek information*

    Observe/Look/Listen

    B. *Knock*

    Go to God

    Go to another or others

    C. *Ask*

    For information/Advice/Ideas

    For Cooperation or Company

    For Understanding or Consideration

    For Opportunity or Forgiveness

    D. Make a Simple Specific Plan

    Tell yourself the truth and affirm yourself

    Consider Thinking/Approaching/Responding Differently

    Consider Kegels/Breathing/Nutrients/Food/Meds/Sleep/Activity

Write it down and set alarm as a reminder to help you remember to take nutrients or medication.

Proceed with the Plan

2. IDENTIFY **External** Stimuli/Situations that Trigger Certain Emotions

A. Seek information

Observe

Listen to Understand

Ask Questions/Acknowledge Situation/Facts

B. Knock

Go to God

Go to another or others

C. Ask

For information/Advice/Ideas

For Cooperation or Company

For Understanding or Consideration

For Opportunity or Forgiveness

D. Make a Simple Specific Plan

Tell yourself the truth and affirm yourself

Consider Thinking/Approaching/Responding Differently

Consider Kegels/Breathing/Nutrients/Food/Meds/Sleep/Activity

Write it down and set alarm as a reminder to help you remember

Proceed with the Plan

Here are some communication formulas we can follow to help deal with negative emotions:

1 Step Communication Examples:

I'm feeling hangry.

I'm feeling frustrated.

I need understanding.

2 Step Communication Examples:

1. I feel _______ (feeling word). I like when_____.
2. I need or would like ______. Would you be willing to _____?

4-Step Communication Formula Example

1. I feel frustrated.
2. I like when the house is kept clean because it helps me function better and have less anxiety.
3. I need help keeping the house clean.
4. Would you be willing to put things back where they belong? Or would you be willing to help me establish a home for certain items that we can agree on?

4-step Communication Formula Example with a Response

1. I feel sad.
2. I like when you think the best of me.
3. I need understanding.
4. Would you be willing to listen to understand what I am saying.

Response Example

Yes.

I need some time to calm down and get something to eat first.

Do you mind if we talk about this after supper? That will help me listen better.

Simple Communication Strategy Example

I see you ____ (hitting yourself).

I hear the ____________ (frustration) in your voice.

I think you might need ______ (a break).

Is that what you need?

Simple Communication Strategy Examples

I like when you _______ (inform me of your plans).

Would you mind ______ (keeping me informed?)

Would you mind ______ (if I ask you a question about your plans?)

I feel included and not as anxious when I know what your plans are.

I'm thinking you are thinking ______________. Is that what you're thinking?

I'm thinking you are feeling ______________. Is that what you're feeling?

I'm thinking you are saying or needing _________. Am I correct?

Checking with others about what they are thinking and feeling, helps to minimize misunderstanding and reduces the occurrence of negative feelings, or more negative feelings.

Finally, creating and proclaiming effective thought patterns out-loud will help to reach your goals and optimal health. Choose the thoughts you think will help to manage the emotions of yourself and others.

Examples of healthy thought patterns:

I am responsible for my thoughts, and responses.

I speak well of others and practice positive self-talk.

I open myself to humor, friendship, and love.

I am understanding and kind and help others when I can.

Without blaming, I express myself honestly.

I allow others to be who they are.

I'm responsible for my life and choices.

I let go of hurts, allow myself to grieve, and move forward.

I let go of negative habit patterns.

I take responsibility for myself and allow others to do the same.

I think before I respond. I serve others when I can do so with a smile.

I seek and attract mutually satisfying relationships with family and friends.

I create win/win solutions with others.

I communicate, clearly, honestly, and lovingly with others.

I ask for what I want and need with ease.

I think on whatever is true, lovely, and praiseworthy.

www.ingramcontent.com/pod-product-compliance
Lightning Source LLC
LaVergne TN
LVHW011050110826
845149LV00015B/3444

9780999477281